RED MOON

SILVER CIRCLE WITCHES

BOOK ONE

ERZABET BISHOP & GINA KINCADE

NAUGHTY NIGHTS PRESS LLC• CANADA

RED MOON RISING

SILVER CIRCLE WITCHES

BOOK ONE

COPYRIGHT © 2021

ERZABET BISHOP & GINA KINCADE

ISBN: 978-1-77357-448-6

978-1-77357-449-3

PUBLISHED BY NAUGHTY NIGHTS PRESS LLC

COVER ART BY KING COVER DESIGNS

RED MOON RISING

A witch trying to forget.

Kate Caeli was very happy with her life, thank you very much. She'd successfully opened Enchanted Yarns and spent most of her time drowning out the memories of her first love with romance novels, stabby knitting needles, and her very successful naughty crochet class. But when one of her shop girls goes missing, it might be up to her to put things right. Even if it means endangering her own life and getting scorched by an old flame.

An ocelot drawn to remember.

When Detective Devi Graves is pulled back to her old stomping grounds, her beast knows something is wrong. But when she catches the scent of her mate at a crime scene, she almost goes off the deep end. Witches are turning up missing and dead, and if she doesn't solve this case quick, the past she longs for will be lost forever. If she isn't careful, it could be more than just her life on the line. Some secrets from the past should be left buried.

DEDICATION

For my hubby and fur babies. I love you
more than words can say.

To Gina... you kick my backside and
keep me reaching for the stars.

For Roseanne. I miss you. Covid took
you too soon.

RED MOON RISING

CHAPTER ONE

BARE BRANCHES OF the tree line dotted the twilight sky. A brisk autumn breeze blew past and Kendall shivered. She huddled next to her car for warmth, but it wasn't helping. The acrid smell of burning leaves tickled her nose. Mischief ran freely in the air tonight. She could sense it. Not much longer until

Samhain. Just another month or so. Time enough before the Witch's Ball for her to make a bit of cash to get her costume in order.

The swamp lay silent, save for the chirp of an occasional cricket and animals running in the brush. She had to get to the Enchanted Yarns shop and soon, even though she really wasn't in the mood tonight. Endless hours winding skeins of yarn and teaching women to wield crochet hooks and knitting needles tended to fray her nerves.

Especially the gaggle of project women that always seemed to show up on Wednesday mornings. They brought their misshapen toilet paper cozies and whatever weird thing Kate had set up for the month; but for the last three weeks, she swore not one hook actually hooked. Clueless, the lot of them. She'd never seen a bunch of women take hours to accomplish absolutely nothing. Well, except make her miserable and drink the shop out of iced tea.

She'd also promised Kate she would show her how to start up her Tiktok account. The witch had many talents, but wielding a phone wasn't one of them.

"Unbelievable," she muttered to herself. Her nerves were still smarting after one of them had complained to Kate, her boss, that she had given them attitude. Kate had rolled her eyes and dealt with the woman, but she was pretty certain the discussion wasn't over. Talk about the last freaking thing she needed.

What was it with busy body women

anyway?

Damned Karens were taking over the world and she was sick of it.

Her mother and Kate were in the same coven. She was more than capable at setting up her own curses, thank you very much. She didn't need help. The bitch had better watch her step the next time she came into the shop. Spit might not be the only thing she needed to worry about being in her tea.

Kendall let out a throaty laugh that echoed in the silent dirt clearing. She'd been here often enough for raves, but tonight, it felt especially creepy. If it got out she was foraying into the swamp, it would put her on the naughty list for sure. But the exhilaration of dancing with the forbidden was a siren song.

A twig snapped in the distance and

her head popped up, eyes searching the darkness.

"Okay. This isn't a serial killer special here. WTF? Dude, I have to go." She stomped her foot and checked her phone for the time. She wanted to get this meeting over with. Her girlfriend, Cybelle, was pissed at her for going, especially knowing she had work first. They planned on looking through the costume shop site once she got paid. After weeks of nothing, a bite on her ad came through. She texted the client she would meet him after her shift at Cast Two Stitches.

Things were lean and she needed the cash. Spell work for hire. Pretty straight forward.

A love spell.

A banishing or two.

No biggie.

What she didn't like was meeting random weirdoes in the swamp after dark. She'd promised Cybelle this would be the last time. Maybe there was someplace safer. She'd have to think on it. There was that park near Lucia's Botanical Brewery. Nobody would mess with her there.

Yeah.

Maybe.

But right now, she was stuck here. The guy had better fucking hurry or she was going to be three shades of late to work.

Kate would kill her if she knew. So would her mom, for that matter. The coven kept harping about not going out alone. Someone was picking off witches and it wasn't safe.

Get real.

If something happened, she could scream, and somebody would come running.

Well, probably.

There was always someone out here getting up to no good. Besides, whoever it was had better keep his hands to himself. She just wasn't in the mood.

The news reported another murder a few days ago. Kendall wasn't worried. She felt around in her pocket, palming the spelled pepper spray she kept on her for just these occasions.

It paid to have insurance.

Shit. She ought to just sell that.

Maybe she could nab the asshole and get the reward the cops had offered. That would shut her mother and the rest of the coven up. She totally knew how to handle herself, thank you very much.

Her stomach growled and she flipped her long black hair out of her eyes impatiently. This guy had kept her here twenty minutes already. She should have stopped by the drive-in on her way, but she wanted to grab some Chinese take-out after work with Cybelle. Or hell, even some pancakes would be good.

The wind cut through her thin outfit, and she let out a curse. She had to dress the part, but jeez. The temperature was dropping and she really wanted to get back in her car and leave.

"Damn, I should have brought a coat." Kendall ground out. Her long black dress and clunky shoes did little to stave off the chill. She rubbed her hands along her arms to try and gather some warmth.

"Okay. Anytime now." Kendall scanned the growing darkness.

So beautiful.

So quiet.

She missed coming here. Used to be, she'd come every weekend with her posse. But since graduation everyone had spun off into the four winds.

Everyone but her.

Kendall sighed. She would get the money she needed to move to New York with Cybelle. It was all they talked about. Freedom. A life without people telling them what to do.

Goddess, she couldn't wait to tell the coven to suck her big toe and like it. But until then, she had to go along to get along. And that meant not getting caught sneaking out here.

The timing was pretty much right on

with her needing costume money. At least, it would have been if the guy had been on time and she wasn't starving. The newly full moon hung bright in the sky and she sensed the pull deep in her bones. Tomorrow night was the coven get together.

So, she should be safe. From what she remembered; the maniac liked to play slasher under the second night of the full moon.

So, yeah.

She'd be fine.

A crackle in the brush to her left startled her, and a warm flush crept over her cheeks. Uh. Probably some rando raccoon digging around for candy wrappers. No more caffeine for her tonight.

Rubbing her arms, Kendall rolled her

eyes and checked her phone.

The blare of a Tiktok video jolted her, but she quickly switched over to her account and checked for new followers.

She had three.

Score.

More followers meant more sales and, praise the goddess, she was tired of working retail. More customers buying spells would bring her the freedom she needed to have her own life.

And she was going to do it, too.

Something shifted in the air, and the scent of sulfur made her wrinkle her nose. "Ewww."

In the darkness to her left a light flickered. Kendall turned her gaze and found the dark form of a large canine bounding out of the tree line.

Night time at the swamp was freaky.

No doubt about it.

She started and backed up a step, and the creature faltered, its eyes narrowing in on her.

Okayyyy.

Maybe it was somebody's dog that snapped his chain. If that was the case, maybe she could get a reward.

The idea appealed.

But damn...it was a really big dog and it didn't look friendly. Not in the least.

What the hell was it?

A Great Dane?

No.

Squinting, she tried to figure it out, but the shadows were too deep. She took a step forward, her nerves jumping around in her stomach.

Something didn't feel right.

A low growl came out of the darkness.

"Jeez boy. Are you okay?" Kendall took a step back as the dog started toward her.

This wasn't good.

She stumbled backward, nearly tripping on the uneven terrain between her and her car. Then, the beast leapt at her. Holding her keys between her fingers, she clawed at the creature, nailing it in the forearm.

It didn't stop it, even for a moment.

"Holy shit, dog. Get *off*." She shoved at him, but he was too strong.

This was anything but a dog.

Her footing unbalanced, she struggled to distance herself.

"Oh, my gawd!" Hot breath tinged with spittle hit her neck and a strangled yelp rang from her lips.

Why weren't her legs working?

She needed to run.

Shit!

"Stop! *Stooooppp*! *Noooooo!*" The wolfen face was twisted, the eyes manic as the jaws opened and snapped against her cheek. This wasn't a werewolf. They were sentient. She'd hung out with some in this very spot. This...this thing was in a blood rage.

Kendall stumbled, and the creature knocked her against the car. The fetid breath blew warm into her face. Kendall reached for her spell bag, but she was too slow. Grabbing a hold of the strap, the beast tore it from her. A bottle of potion burst, letting loose a spell of confusion.

Shit!

The creature slipped and fell to the

side, shaking its head, allowing her a brief window of escape. Kendall darted off beneath the canopy of moss and half dead trees, running like the hounds of Hell were after her.

Branches and twigs snapped as she burst through the brush. She strained to see in the inky darkness. Clouds covered the moon, snuffing out what little light she had.

There.

Something in the distance.

A soft light glowed through the trees and she gave a sob of relief. She ran toward it.

Someone was there.

Maybe they could help.

Her feet pounded against the ground, her breath hard and fast in her ears. Behind her she heard the beast making progress.

The source of the illumination came from a small clearing.

Shit.

The rave site.

No wonder it looked familiar. Maybe someone was there. A witch who could help her.

Kendall burst through the trees, and skidded to a stop. This wasn't a rave. Not by a long shot.

A form stood in the center of a crudely drawn pentagram gouged into the earth. Behind her, two golden moon shaped scythes stood at attention on either side of what appeared to be an altar.

There, a woman stood, her back to Kendall. The suit she wore was expensive and her shoes had higher heels than anything she'd ever seen, let alone considered walking in.

"Hello?" Her voice cracked and she cringed. "Can you help me? There's this crazy dog..."

A feminine face turned to face her, only the docile smile she was expecting was replaced by something other.

Something cold and reptilian.

What had she just walked into?

"You're late."

"Do I know you?"

Kendall's brain sputtered and she tried to think. The spell must have gotten on her, because whatever she said wasn't making sense.

"You're selling, my dear. And I'm buying."

"No..." she stuttered. "I mean, I was supposed to meet this guy out here for a spell."

"And so, you have."

"You?" Kendall rasped. "I don't understand." The sulfur smell was nearly overpowering now and she almost gagged.

A flash of silver emerged from the woman's suit.

"Some things are not meant for you."

Kendall swung around to run. The beast countered her movements, blocking her way. Its yellow eyes glowed in the darkness. She never felt the blade enter. Only the sensation of falling as the ground rose up to meet her, and the slow exsanguination of her blood as it left her body and filled the pentagram.

CHAPTER TWO

"NO, JESSICA. YOU hook it like this." Gripping the scarlet sport weight yarn in her hand, Kate maneuvered the hook until the stitch came out just right. "Class, I want you to all take out your phones and look up how to do a single crochet stitch. It's on my channel. But if you need a refresher, here goes."

An abandoned crochet hook took off from the long brown folding table and found an extra skein of yarn.

"Up we go!"

The hook twirled in midair, showing the stitch in question multiple times until it had made its round to all the ladies.

Goddess, was this what her magic was reduced to these days? Kate sighed and pasted a smile on her face.

"How do we do that?" One of the older ladies grumbled.

"You Tube, Marge."

"I'd rather be able to wiggle my nose and pull that off."

"Sorry, hon. Nose wiggling will only get you so far. Trust me." Kate winked and let the ladies get back to their projects.

Nine distinct grumbles ensued, but the women laughed and pulled out their androids and iPhones, linking to the Internet.

She didn't mind pulling the witch card sometimes. It felt good to at least put her powers to some kind of use. These days, she didn't much make it to the town coven meetings. Instead, she relied on a once-a-month brew with her inner circle and tonight was the night.

"Excellent. This is one of the best ways to watch and learn. Repeat after me. Videos are my friend."

A chorus of feminine voices echoed her own and everyone began to laugh.

"Kate, you kill me." Jessica grinned, holding up the bikini top she had been working on for the last two weeks. "Did you post it on Tiktok, too?"

"Last night. I was on there for hours."

And she had been. If Kendall had shown up to help her set everything up, it would have gone off without a hitch. As it was, she'd spent a ton of time trying to master what the girl had told her.

Lighting.

Music.

Pictures that pop.

Hashtags.

It was a whole new world—and a world that was all Kendall's idea.

"I use it for my side business, Kate. More followers equal more sales and we all need more sales."

The girl wasn't wrong.

But the fact that she hadn't shown up wasn't like her. And she hadn't come in for her shift today, either.

No calls.

No texts.

Nothing.

She'd been a little fidgety lately, but hadn't seemed the type to just bail on her. Sliding her phone out of her back pocket, Kate frowned. Still no return calls or texts.

Closing her eyes, she reached for the girl's name badge, left on the back counter, and let her senses reach out.

Where are you?

Nothing but darkness greeted Kate and she frowned. Making her way toward the chair behind her computer, she sat down and eased the door shut between the class and her private space. They could still come around the front counter, but all she needed was a moment or two to set her spell in motion.

Her element was air and she would use it to find her missing friend. A spark of an idea formed. It had worked before when she needed to find her coven sisters.

She called the quarters to her, and reveled in her element of air. Wisps of magic floated around her and Kate hummed the simple spell under her breath.

"A simple kiss to find a friend, to thwart all mischief to an end."

The kiss blown, she smiled as it rattled the door on its way out into the night.

"Goddess help her if she's just playing hooky."

A loud burst of laughter from the group brought her focus back.

Kate eased the door open and checked her watch. Only ten minutes left in class.

Jessica was grimacing and working on a troublesome stitch.

"You got it?"

"I think so."

"Well, if you get lost, just bring up one of the videos. Just be careful not to fall in."

Jessica laughed. "I know. I went to look up a gardening hack and four hours later, Hyacinth asked me what was for dinner. Whoops."

"You're telling me. It's worse than YouTube."

Grimacing, Jessica nodded. "So true."

Kate turned toward the group.

"Okay, gang. The project list for this month includes a wrist cuff pattern or a simple headband for you ladies who don't want to frighten the fish, so to speak." Kate smiled as the group began to titter with laughter. "The project models are up on the board for you to see. Personally, I think the black and pink ones are wicked cool."

"Kate?" A young redhead in the back of the room stood up.

"Yes, Arlene."

"Can you help me with last month's project? I can't seem to get this right at all." Arlene held up a gray vibrator cozy that was supposed to be rectangular but had somehow gone horribly wrong.

"Oh wow, honey. What have you done?" Joan, a woman in her mid-forties asked, holding up her own completed project.

"Remember that little scarf you made

last Christmas, Joan? Don't judge." Kate raised her eyebrows and smiled. "Can you see if you can help Arlene figure out where her stitches went wonky while I get everyone checked out?"

"Sure." Joan slid her chair down and the two began comparing notes.

"Thanks." Kate glanced around the room. Ladies were poking through some of the new wools and synthetics she had brought back with her from market. Others were at the back of the room in the kitchen sampling the iced tea and cookies she had prepared while they decided what naughtiness they were going to work on.

"Okay class, decide which project you want to start and I'll be around to talk with you about yarn selection. For anyone interested in next month's pattern, we're going to work on a matching lacy nightie and a sleeping mask."

Kate made her way to the back of the class and watched the ladies race to the project board and signup sheet. Naughty Crochet had to be her most popular class night ever. She had sunk her life savings into this shop and was determined to offer something a bit different than the average doilies and baby sweaters most of the local yarn stores offered.

"Ladies, don't forget to take your measurements for next month. You're going to need them for the sizing."

Kate didn't even bother to listen to the griping her announcement prompted. She understood. Not a slim woman, she flinched whenever she had to get on a scale, measure body parts, or go shopping. Her best moments were in her head and through her crochet hook.

Not to even mention her stash of smut novels. It was her secret joy and every night after work, she retreated into the bedroom with a glass of wine, her latest erotic pick, and her sketchpad. It was how most of her projects had been born.

Her thoughts drifted and she couldn't wait to close shop and get over to Lucia's. But she couldn't stop thinking about Kendall.

Twenty minutes at the register and the shop was empty. With a smile, she snagged her purse off the back counter and reached for her keys. She could already taste one of Lucia's brews now.

She let her senses reach out for a

trace of the tracking spell, but it was still searching.

Odd.

A flick of her wrist and the door was locked and armed behind her and she headed off into the night, unaware that a pair of eyes watched her from the darkness.

CHAPTER THREE

IT WAS TOO quiet.

That was the first thing Detective Devi Graves noticed as she stepped out of the parked car and into the alley. Normally, a crime scene would be bustling with cops and forensic techs. She looked up at the sky and grimaced. She'd gotten the orders from her captain to head back to her hometown in Bixby, Texas. If it hadn't been for Avery, she would have just kept going.

Too much witch and shifter politics. She preferred to live on her own merits and not bound to some old-fashioned idea of what was normal in the witching world.

What about her world?

Better yet, what about Kate's?

She didn't want to tie the other woman down by dragging her around the country investigating the weird shit that always seemed to fall in her lap. Always on loan to some police department or another, she hadn't called one place home since she'd left.

Seven years.

It felt longer.

They'd been good, but the tiniest part

of her wondered when things were going to settle down. She usually shoved that thought down into the dark places she didn't think about, but lately, it had been rearing its head more and more often.

So had thoughts of Kate.

She missed her.

Her smell.

Her taste.

Her laugh.

Her.

She also didn't want to be forced into a relationship because Kate was a witch and she was supposed to follow suit and be her familiar.

It wasn't in her plan.

But here she was, driving right back into the hornet's nest.

Familiar landmarks dotted the

highway, and her gut tightened with every mile. She would have driven right past the old diner but a text shot through from her old boss and mentor, stopping her in her tracks.

Shit.

She pulled into the dark parking lot and tried to push down the nausea. Popping a couple of papaya tablets, she parked the rental away from the road.

The sky was clear with no clouds. She hated full moons. In her line of work, that meant the whole world usually went ape shit, taking her along for the ride. It was true now more than ever.

Devi took in the dark alley and her nostrils flared. Disgusted, she took a step backward.

It smelled of blood and death. Her

inner beast coiled, ready to break free, and she had to dig her nails into her arm to still the urge. Now was not the time. She pressed her hand against the blade hidden in her pocket and sucked in a breath.

Corny and stereotypical, but it was the faith and the meaning behind it that tied her to the spelled knife. That was enough. Kate had matching daggers made for them. With every touch, she felt her power curl around her like a caress and it eased her loneliness.

"What the hell?" Her gaze darted up from the black pool of blood shimmering in the light of the moon and the impersonal glare of the streetlights. Gore streaked across the concrete toward the hazy red glow emanating from the back exit of the diner. It was propped open.

Hmmm. In this side of town, you kept your doors locked and your ass to the wall if you had to be out after dark.

"That's what I was hoping you could tell me." Detective Sergeant Avery stepped out of the shadows, a grim expression on his too pale face. His white and gray hair lay messily on his head, like he'd been running his hand through it. He only did that when his back was against the wall.

Police tape fluttered in the early morning breeze, the unis keeping the few stragglers at bay. "Thanks for coming."

Thinning salt and pepper hair and a weary expression tugged at her heart. It had been too long. He was the reason she'd gotten this job. Like a father, he'd been there for her when her world had fallen apart and had nudged her in the right direction to help her get her shit together.

She just wasn't sure why exactly he'd felt the need to call her back.

Devi peered into the shadows, but things blacker than night would be staring back at this hour of the morning so she refocused her attention to the task at hand.

Lucky me.

Something skittered down her spine and she felt a niggle of fear and awareness.

"Who was it?" She knew most of the officers and detectives that worked the streets of Bixby, but three years was a long time.

Avery looked down at the concrete smear and swallowed. "James," his voice broke. "It was James."

Goddess.

He'd been her first partner when she'd barely cut her teeth at the department.

"Shit." She glared up at her. "What was he doing out here without backup?"

"He had backup. He just didn't use it." A blonde woman in nose bleed heels made her way into the alley, her eyes red and her face blotchy. The rest of her was as polished as it got. Hair pulled into a tight ponytail, not a strand out of place. Her suit jacket crisp over a white button-down shirt and dress jeans, she looked like she'd just come from a night out instead of wading through a crime scene.

"Graves, this is Cappelli. She and James were partners."

She couldn't help but size her up and the other woman knew it, judging by the way her eyes narrowed.

Devi gave her a courtesy nod. "Where?"

"Follow me."

Devi trailed behind Cappelli as she made her way down the back alley, avoiding the congealing pools of blood, her heels clacking against the wooden floor as she entered the building. The place was much like she remembered it. Permanently stuck in the fifties, the décor was faded, the band posters dated, and the worn booths cracked and peeling.

Absently, she wondered when it had closed. The scent of old grease and salt warred with the sickly-sweet aroma of blood and other things. Devi tried to breathe through her mouth before she gagged.

CSI techs began to roll in. The scene was getting busier than she liked. Avery stood in the doorway, a haggard expression on his face. "I wouldn't have bothered you, but this one needed your particular...expertise. You knew him."

Cappelli gave her a cold stare and continued into the recesses of the diner.

The acrid scent of familiar demon magic met Devi's nose and her animal hissed, ears flattening.

I know.

Demon magic had its consequences. James must have found that out the hard way. But she wasn't going to say it. Not yet. She'd helped him to contain it once, but judging from the carnage, he hadn't listened.

Avery nodded and stared past her into the room. The diner looked like any other, save for the trail of blood that came through the doorway. Tired linoleum and worn fixtures made up the scene. She had spent hours in places just like this wherever she landed. The prices were cheap and the grease flowed easy.

She narrowed her eyes and moved past Avery and Cappelli into the main part of the room, mindful of her steps. Her boots barely made a sound. The trail of blood stopped in front of a worn wooden booth with cracked red vinyl seats. There, on the tablem was a small wooden box, a sinister glow coming from the small space where the lid had been haphazardly replaced and not sealed.

"What the hell?" Devi's heart thudded in her chest.

Fuck.

She knew that box.

It had been the center of most of her nightmares since her parents had been killed when she was a girl.

Her familial history had been dotted with ocelots tied to demons or witches that harnessed demon power. Most of them hadn't lived long, but once you have a demon on your tail, you were screwed. And that fucking box was supposed to be buried in consecrated ground.

Again.

Cappelli cleared her throat. "He said he was taking this box to someone. Someone who would know what to do with it. He'd found it under his house last month."

"Last month?"

Cappelli nodded.

That was a load of horseshit. She'd helped him bury it before she left town. Under his house, in sanctified earth.

Why the fuck did he mess with it?

The damn thing had almost killed him before.

Now it looked like it had succeeded.

"Have things been..." Devi paused, thinking. "More active in town than normal?"

"What are you driving at, detective?" Cappelli asked.

"I'm saying this thing reeks of demon magic and I don't even have to touch it."

Cappelli's brow furrowed. "What?"

Devi sighed. Goddess, but she hated explaining herself. And she really, really didn't want to.

It was James' secret.

Not hers.

"Graves has some unique talents that have come in handy over the years." Avery said. "I knew something was off, but..."

She didn't want to touch the damned thing, but until she did, they were going to be in the dark. She'd kill him, but he was already dead.

Damn it.

Sadness for her friend and the detective he'd been swirled in her gut. He'd found the box at an antique market. It had looked like a good find, but when he'd gotten the chance to open it, the reality was a whole other thing.

The residue was there, but she wasn't sure if the demon was still lurking inside or if it had flown to the four winds.

"Stand back."

Goddess, but she didn't want to do

this.

Devi took a step forward and let her finger trail along the top of the lid. Visions crowded in the way they always did and she almost cried out.

Clutching the table, she broke her connection to the box and staggered toward a booth and threw herself down.

Visions of her helping James bury the box beneath his house circled in her mind.

The holy water.

The demon vowing vengeance.

He had kept it the crawl space with the promise that he'd never open it again after she helped him seal it.

He hadn't listened.

Nightmares plagued him. He couldn't sleep. And then one night he found himself standing just outside the crawl space, dirt all over his pajamas.

The demon had worn him down until he went a step further and dug the box up. It belonged to the demon that had taken his life and ripped it all to hell. No one, not even Avery or Cappelli had known about it. At least, nothing he hadn't wanted them to know.

But when the demon's face was revealed, she almost threw up. Some mistakes never left you and this was one.

Instead of having him bury the thing, she should have burned the box and sent the bitch back to Hell where she belonged.

Devi's nails curled into her palms and she struggled to keep her ocelot reined in. Her beast wanted to run, to escape the sulfurous death that coated the place like a bad paint explosion.

James had been lying. Not just to his partner, but Avery as well.

Not something she wanted to reveal.

Yet.

The box, its lid still askew, oozed an energy that made her want to alternatively sink inside of it and burn it to a cinder. There was a power that played on people's worst and best intentions, and she knew it firsthand.

The only question was, why bring it here?

If it had been nestled under his house, what made him think he could contain the force inside of it?

Had he been dealing with a local witch?

Goddess, she hoped not.

"Who was he supposed to meet? He

brought it here for a purpose."

"I don't know."

"Was he acting strange? Secretive?" Devi prodded.

Cappelli looked her square in the eye. "I know James must have had his reasons for coming here but he didn't tell me about it. As to being secretive? Well, let's just say we both led different lives and leave it at that."

Oh. Snap.

"Well, that's less than helpful."

"What do you want? A fucking roadmap? Someone killed my partner. Probably a witch. You're from around here, so you know better than anyone just how low they'll go to get the upper hand."

Her animal growled low, but she coughed and shook it off. Throat punching the bitch wasn't going to help the situation, and right now she answered to James before anybody else.

Frowning, she looked closer at the box.

Why had James moved it?

It just didn't make sense. To Cappelli's point, the witches in Bixby had always been a little power hungry. That was one of the things that drove her to leave.

The other had been buried in that fucking box.

"Ya'll might want to move back a few steps."

Devi reached for a shaker of table salt. Uncapping it, she made a circle around the box, then snagged a fork and edged the lid the rest of the way off.

The box was pulsing with rancid

power. Ice sluiced down the back of her spine as she felt the residual energy emanating from the glow. Demon still there or not, it was creepy as fuck.

She'd hated the thing from the first moment James showed it to her. He'd been so excited, but when he uncovered it in the trunk of his car, she'd taken one look at it and backed away.

"What the hell did you buy that for?" she'd said.

God, the sweet idiot had the indecency to look hurt.

"I needed something for my remotes."

"You're a cop. How could you not sense that thing is evil?"

His eyes, now snapping with anger, met hers. "Well, I guess we can't all be as in tune with the freaky shit as you are."

Then, he slammed the trunk shut and didn't say another thing about it. But two weeks later, he'd shown up at her apartment and begged her to help him get rid of it.

And here they were.

Dark laughter echoed through the room and Devi suddenly wished she'd made the circle just a little bit bigger.

Oh fuck.

Oh fuck. Oh fuck.

People who played with demons thought it was a fun thing until a real one showed up. She knew that first hand. Everyone in the room was at risk.

She shoved Avery and Cappelli toward the door.

"Get everyone out. Now."

Cappelli's eyes met hers and awareness made her eyes snap hard.

"Fix it," she hissed. "James was my partner. It can't go down this way."

"He was mine too. Once."

Without another word, she pushed her way out the back door, ordering the technicians outside until further notice.

Devi closed her eyes, her stomach knotting up in a combination of nerves and her impending change. She would have to fuck with her on a full moon. All she could do is try and keep her wits about her. As if she could do anything else.

She was going to have to talk to Avery about his unfortunate timing. It was hard to do human shit when you had an over eager ocelot trying to claw her way out of her skin when they had a standing appointment.

Full moons sucked.

Red eyes glowed out of the shadows of the box and a dark chuckle laced with hellfire curdled the air. A familiar form took shape, her smooth features framing eyes that burned bright in the murky darkness of the diner.

"You."

"Hello, pet. No, wait..." The demon held up one elegantly manicured finger and swirled it through a puddle of blood that had congealed on the table. Bringing to her lips, she licked it off, savoring the flavor. "That would be, detective now, wouldn't it? What do they call a familiar afraid of getting a little too close to the fire?" She elegantly wiped at her mouth with a paper napkin. "Ummm. Nothing like a little terror to make it zing. Don't you agree?"

Devi growled, her cat waiting for the

change to push her way through. The bitch had fucked with her once. She wouldn't let her do it again.

"What are you doing here?"

"Oh...catching up on some unfinished business. How about you?"

"Right. Now, how's about you get back in the box so we can call it a day?"

"Oh...I'm not quite done yet."

"I think you are." The blade in her pocket burned bright and she longed to just bury it in her and light the whole thing on fire.

"How is the moon tonight, Devi? Do you find it scintillating?" The demon's eyes burned bright as she sashayed toward her, swinging her hips with every step. The maroon suit would have looked ridiculous on just about anyone else, but with her chestnut hair and curvaceous build, Gambian was able to pull it off and look damn sexy in the process.

It was also a ruse.

"Your old partner... James, was it?" The demon paused, deliberately avoiding another puddle of blood that streaked down the floor. "He dug the box up for you. How quaint." She glanced over at Devi, her blood red lips curving up into an evil smile.

"For me? Now why would he do that?"

Unless she'd been spinning lies.

Gambian chuckled, her laughter making the hair on Devi's arms stand at attention. "He knew we had unfinished business, you and I. Well...we are practically related. Our families have been working together for centuries. It's only right I made you see just how wrong you were by running off to play detective."

"Fuck you."

"Ah. Now that's the spitfire I remember so well. And I thought that insipid Kate ruined you forever."

"Don't talk about Kate," Devi ground out, her jaw locking in frustration.

"Whyever not? You're not still together, are you? I thought you had higher aspirations than being someone's pet kitty?"

She sauntered closer, kicking something that squelched out of her way.

Devi wasn't going to answer.

"Oh, come on now. Don't be a spoil sport. You know I'll have to make sure you come to the right decision, don't you?"

"Leave me alone."

"Oh, my dear. Didn't you know? Your parents made sure our bond could never be broken."

She held up a tiny vial of what looked like blood.

"What the fuck is that?"

"Our future."

"Bullshit," Devi spat the word. There was no future with a demon. Her parents had shown her that.

The hard way.

"Don't take my word for it." Gambian waved the vial at her, then snatched it back. "I know you can touch and tell. But break it and well...I'll just have to fill it again, won't I?"

"You wish."

"Oh, I do." Gambian placed the vial on the table between them and stood back, waiting.

Touching anything from the demon wasn't in her wheelhouse. But if it was her blood, surely, she'd know just by being close to it.

Closing her eyes, she let her hand hover over the table, getting as close as she could without actually touching the vial.

Faint images filtered through her senses, but the one that lingered the most was her mother drawing the blood, and the pain in her arm from the incision. She still had a half moon scar there. A mark.

"Oh yes. You see it now, don't you?"

Bile rose up Devi's throat and she pushed away from the table, the images evaporating like they'd never been.

"Was it true?" She hadn't meant to ask, but it tumbled out before she could stop herself. Asking a demon any question was a bad idea.

But she already knew.

It was her blood.

"I don't hold with a contract I didn't make."

"Well now...that isn't entirely true, is it? I have your blood right here to make sure you keep up with your end of the bargain."

"No."

"No?" Gambian laughed, her eyes twinkling with delight. "Now, that's just what your friend here told me when he dug me out of the hole you put me in. Seven years is a long time, kitty cat."

"I haven't changed my mind. Not then. Not now."

"Well, then. We'll just have to see how long you intend to be stubborn. Witches love parties. And I have several planned for the next few hours. I do hope you can attend."

Gambian wrapped herself around Devi, pressing herself against her. Her teeth grazed against her throat, fangs dragging across her flesh carving little rivulets of blood in their wake. Her hands caressed her, cupping her through her clothes.

"You know you want this. I know you better than anyone else ever will."

Devi swayed, the soft curves of her breasts molding themselves to her curves as Gambian pushed her against the wall. The sour smell of rot left from her earlier carnage brought her back to herself.

"No!" She shoved her away, gasping for air, willing her body back under control.

She loved Kate.

Even if she had to leave her behind to protect her.

"That was not wise, Devi." Storms brewed behind the demon's eyes. Power skittered in the shadows and her dark hair moved with unseen wind. "You have something of mine and I will take it."

"What are you talking about?" Devi searched her memory for acceptable spells that would banish her back into the box, but her mind would not focus. The siren's call of the moon rippled through her body and she began to lose control as her muscles contracted and began to reform.

Shit.

Not now.

Her cat screamed, coaxed to the

surface by Gambian.

No.

She wants to control you.

Stay.

Please.

Devi bent over, gasping as she fought the change with everything she had.

"Did you think I would let you leave me in that box? James is dead because you wouldn't take your place."

"No."

"How many more have to die before you accept your fate? You belong to me, pet. And I won't take no for an answer." She scooped up the blood-filled vial and it vanished into her suit pocket.

There had to be a way to toss the bitch back to the bowels of Hell. She just had to find it.

Clutching the table, Devi grabbed the

salt and pried open the spout with shaking hands.

"No means no. I'll put you back in that box a hundred times for what you did to me and my parents. Not to mention James." She flung the salt in an arc, and the demon howled.

Gambian screamed. "You dare!"

"I dare anything to keep my people safe."

"The night isn't over. We'll be seeing each other again soon."

"I'm counting on it." With that, she dug a surprise of her own from her pocket, but before she could douse the demon with holy water, the bitch had vanished into the night.

CHAPTER FOUR

DEVI KNEW THEY were close to the crime scene by the people gathering in the street. Nothing ever happened on the privileged side of town. Tragedy was for someone else. Someone less fortunate. She could read the confusion in the wide stares of the neighbors as she and her very temporary partner got out of the car and made their way up the driveway to the uniform on scene.

Gambian had promised she would be busy, and so far, she was racking up the bodies.

One crime scene down, and already a second one. She gazed up at the moon, wincing. When this was over, she owed her cat a run in the woods. No creeps. No demons. Just her and a damn good run. But for now, she was still on loan and desperate to find Gambian before she destroyed every witch in Bixby until she got to Kate. And that wasn't going to happen.

"Officer." Cappelli reached him first and flashed her badge. Devi followed close behind, grinding her teeth. The woman had the personality of a wet dishrag and she was grinding it in that it was her town, her case.

Fine.

Let her try and put a roundish demon in a square box—again—and see how that went.

Speaking of the box...the damn thing was in the trunk of Cappelli's car, reeking of sulfur and shooting off enough energy to give her a headache.

With her luck, she'd be here weeks, when all she wanted to do was get home and decompress. Avery told her one night. She didn't believe him.

She left town to protect Kate and leave Gambian behind and being here was messing with her mind. Damn James for digging her up. Things would have been fine if he'd just left well enough alone. Crating that bitch had almost killed her the first time. But it would be worth it again if she could get to her before she got to Kate.

Her thoughts drifted back to the hotel room and images of flopping on the bed and getting some actual sleep taunted her.

Hah.

As if she could sleep.

Not a chance.

She took in the brick facades and coiffed lawns. You'd never know that a mile or so away there was a murder scene. Another witch found with her throat slit in an alley behind a popular coffee chain. Or even that there was one inside the holy sanctum of the pristine suburban sprawl. Well, unless you ignored the flashing lights of the squad cars and uniformed officers.

Things like this just didn't happen in

Bixby, Texas. Especially in neighborhoods like this one. It was time she took the lead, whether little miss tight britches liked it or not. She sped up so she was ahead of Cappelli by the time they got to the edge of the property in question.

"Your business?" The officer's gaunt face was ghost like in the faint light of the flashlight as he flashed the beam in her direction.

Devi flipped open her badge.

"Inside." His voice was firm, but she detected a quaver at the end.

"Bad one?"

"Yes. ma'am." He looked back toward the residence and shivered.

Without a word, Devi lifted the tape and leveraged herself beneath it. Cappelli joined her letting the stark yellow crime scene tape fall back in place. Her gaze locked on the entrance to the house. Sheer curtains covered the windows. She made out shapes of bodies moving inside.

"At it again so soon?" A gruff voice ground out.

"Apparently." Devi hesitated, but he knew she would. Touching people told her too much. That's what made her good at her job. She reached out and took it, the images of what he had just seen rippling through her mind. It was also what made her a great familiar. Magic bonded to her like cheddar powder on popcorn. And old witch that he was, he knew talent when he saw it.

Damn it.

She staggered a little, holding the nausea down. It was getting to her. First the diner, then the alley murder, and now this. That, and the enormity of what they were facing. A demon with a penchant for witches didn't bode well. And the fact that it brought her back to Bixby when she'd done everything in her power to put distance between them, just pissed her off and simultaneously scared the shit out of her.

She fingered her phone and thought about calling her, but squashed the idea like a bug.

Seven years was a long time.

"Sir." Cappelli nodded, missing nothing of the exchange between her supervisor and Devi.

"You, okay?" His steely eyes regarded her; his expression no more moveable than stone. He stepped out of the doorway, light pooling out in the emerging darkness. The scent of blood and spoiled things drifted out behind him.

"So far."

"We left the rental at the diner." And Devi could hear every ounce of resentment curling through her words. The sulfur reek was going to take months to air out.

The evil part of her couldn't help but smile. She could have taken the rental, but what the hell, right? Cappelli wanted to take the reins, she could just take a giant bite out of a shit sandwich and like it.

He nodded once at Cappelli but said nothing.

Devi gave a quick nod. "Where?"

His face twisted. "Come on." He motioned her and Cappelli inside and shut the door behind him as soon as they were through. "The wife is in the back bedroom. The son went missing tonight, and we've heard this may be related to the scene you just left."

"How so?" Cappelli spoke up, the first words she'd uttered since they entered the house.

"The team has been working on identifying the bodies from the alley."

They passed through a living room filled with well-worn furniture. A brown leather couch that had seen better days, a weary looking easy chair and scuffed wooden end tables covered in books filled the space. It was comfortable and homey, with landscape paintings of local art. Dovi stopped when she passed a hall table laden with family photos.

There.

She picked up one of a young man she'd seen just an hour ago, his body strewn about like trash next to the dumpster. He was found next to a young woman dressed like she was going to an all-out Goth witch function.

There hadn't been a familiar present. They were too young. But in some ways that was even worse.

Gambian was racking up the points tonight.

Tears prickled in her eyes. If the son was involved, what did that mean for the rest of the family? She continued down the hall. Cappelli had stopped to discuss something with Avery and another officer. That was fine. She preferred doing what she did alone. And she didn't need the other woman's hostility mixing with the energy of the scene.

The second door down was the boy's bedroom. White walls covered in posters of D&D and Game of Thrones. But there, on his desk, was the clue she'd been expecting to find. A thick, leather-bound tome like one she herself had at home.

Demon Craft: The Summoning.

She ran her fingers over the open pages but the impressions from the pages were faint and didn't tell her much. Leaning forward, she noted the portion he'd been reading.

Blood sacrifice.

How apt.

Darkness called to darkness. And before you knew it, you were lunch.

Bye, bye Felicia.

A clawing in her gut had her moving again. This was one part of the puzzle. The others were here in the house. She gave the room another cursory glance and shut the door behind her. She needed to see the body. Passing through the living room again, she stopped at the crime scene tape. The smell was thick and viscous, and made her already temperamental gut-churn.

Do your job.

Find the answer.

This is what you're here for, no matter the cost to you.

Blood spatter darkened patches of the beige carpet and walls of the dining room, a circular pattern that ended at the closed door in front of her. She made her way around the blood noting the ordinary looking wooden table and bare walls. It was obvious no one ate here.

Devi opened the door and stepped into a dark library. Walls of blood-spattered bookshelves and antiquities that didn't fit into the bland suburban scene staggered her senses.

"My God." It was worse in person. The reek of old blood, dark magic, and vomit assaulted her senses, blending with the stench of death.

The body lay twisted on the floor covered by tan pants and white shirt violated by the blood of unexplainable wounds and puffy welts on the skin.

Bee stings?

Devi bent over the body, trying to keep her boots from stepping in the congealing blood. A dark, elongated wooden object lay askew next to the corpse. She shifted her weight to see it better

Avery appeared at the door, his gaze settling on something across the room. "I don't like it. Wife said he just got back from some weird ass vacation in the middle of the swamp. Then, he locked himself in here."

A buzzing noise wafted through the room. Her fingertips tingled. There. She opened her eyes and her gaze fell on the dark wooden object. She flipped it over with the toe of her boot.

A wooden mask.

She'd seen others like it in the Voodoo shops she'd visited in the past. They made her skin crawl every time. The hollow eye sockets pulsed with shadows and sinister secrets. Her gaze darted around the library, landing on an open box on a nearby table.

She started to touch it, but her animal hissed, forcing her to back up.

"Our boy here must have been

dabbling with the occult." Avery picked up a feathered object with tiny shells dangling from it. He shook the piece, and she could see the gears working in his head, but even he didn't know what he was messing with.

That was why they'd brought her in.

Goddess, what had been happening here?

She'd only been gone seven years.

"Avery, don't touch anything." She glanced around the walls. Most were covered with books, but where there was bare wall space, she found artwork depicting the rise of demons from the depths of Hell and strange landscapes that reminded her of Dante's Inferno. Her gaze rolled over the books on the shelf. Lovecraft, an illustrated Necronomicon, books on the occult both obscure and mainstream.

This is where the money was.

Right here in this room.

She needed to talk to the wife.

"I should get the team in here and get it cleared out. Do you need to look at anything else?" He flipped open his phone, pecked out something, and then slid it back into his pocket.

"No. I don't think so." Devi replied, distracted. "The wife? What's her name?"

"Skyler. Skyler Chambers."

Chambers.

As in The King in Yellow.

Was it a coincidence?

No.

She didn't believe that for one minute.

She left Avery to work with the crime scene crew. She could have touched the body but she didn't have to. He was a willing sacrifice to summon beings that should have remained in another dimension. She reached the last bedroom at the end of the hall. The officer guarding the door opened it, allowing her to pass.

The room was empty save for a queen size bed and dresser; a glass paned door to the outside hung open, letting in the fetid night air. Devi burst into a run, covering the small bedroom in a few steps, her boots hitting the concrete pad outside with a thump. It took a moment for her eyes to adjust to the dark.

The house rested on the edge of the swamp and Skyler Chambers was halfway toward the water's edge. The woman's nightgown glowed white in the gloom, her long blonde hair tumbling to her waist.

"Mrs. Chambers! Wait!" Devi darted forward as the woman proceeded toward the water. "Stop! Please."

The woman turned and regarded Devi with an unreadable expression. "It's time. The dead lie dreaming and they must awake."

"No." Devi panted. "No. Your husband...your son."

"They are with Her now. It's time for a new world." Her gaze met Devi's with a pitying expression. "You will learn to see. I see Her mark on you already." Her hand reached out to touch Devi.

Images both horrifying and glorious tumbled into Devi's mind all at once. Goddesses and dead things and a language so old she could only guess at its meaning.

The death of her husband.

Her boy going leaving for the party with his girlfriend, knowing what his fate would be.

It was all orchestrated.

All planned.

Skyler released Devi and offered her a joyous smile, her fingers sliding down the material of Devi's jacket. "You'll see. Look to the stars. Your blade is ripe for the purpose. Feed it. She is coming, cat. I hope you're ready."

The other woman stepped into the water and slowly sank beneath the waves, her nightgown filling with air as it submerged around her. In moments she was gone save for a smattering of air bubbles. The world was full of silence and the chirping of cicadas.

One step was all it took for her to

follow, and that was what she did. Her ocelot scratched and bit as she found herself half submerged in the fetid water.

In the distance she heard Cappelli calling her name. Devi looked on, powerless to move. As the ripples in the water ceased, a reflection of the night sky and the over-ripe moon came into view. She slipped the blade out of its holster and readied herself as something shifted in the wind and she caught the scent of something that terrified her.

CHAPTER FIVE

SHE SHOULD HAVE driven right to Lucia's, but the whispers in the air tonight felt restless. Kate reached out to her kiss spell, but nothing outright came back. But what she did smell was the poignant scent of sulfur and a tinge of dark magic in the air.

"That's odd."

Kendall's apartment wasn't too far. She roomed with her girlfriend and odds were, she was just being a snowflake.

Pulling into the driveway, she noticed Kendall's car wasn't there.

Minutes later, she was knocking at the door.

"Kendall. Are you in there? It's Kate."

The door swung open and a teary eyed Cybelle peered out at her, the scent of patchouli and smoke drifting out to greet her.

"Kate?"

She nodded. It had been a while since she'd been introduced to the younger woman.

"Hey. I know it's late. I was just wondering if Kendall was here."

"No. I was just going to text you to see if you'd seen her." Cybelle wiped at her eyes. "She hasn't been home since last night when she left to go to work at the shop."

"What?"

But Kendall hadn't shown up.

"Where else did she say she was going?"

Cybelle's lips twisted. "That damned swamp. She's been selling spells on the side to try to get us more money. Some guy was supposed to buy one off her."

Unease slid down her spine.

"And she was going to do this before work?"

"Yeah." Cybelle reached for a cigarette in the pocket of her robe and flicked open a lighter. As she shifted her arm, Kate got a glimpse of a bandage.

"Did you cut yourself?"

Cybelle flinched.

"No." Her eyes darted away and she arranged the robe so it covered the injury. "I just cut it at work. No big deal."

"Okay. Is there any place else she would have gone? You guys...are all right?"

The salty scent of fire and clove cigarettes tickled Kate's nose.

Cybelle shook her head, wrapping her arms around herself. "We're fine. But I'm totally pissed that she went out there."

Kate hadn't been to the swamp in years. Not since...Devi. Goddess, just thinking about her gouged out a new hole in her heart. She missed her so much.

But she wasn't going to think about her. Not now. The connection in their blood was bad enough, she didn't need to actively pull it up to torture herself.

Kendall was her worry now. Devi was a ghost from the past that just needed to stay there. If someone doesn't want to stay, you can't make them. Goddess, but she hoped Cybelle wasn't about to experience that loss.

"I'll see what I can find out."

Cybelle took a puff of her cigarette and held it between shaking fingers.

"Thanks. I'd appreciate it."

Without a word, Kate headed for her car. With any luck, her sister witches would have some ideas. Her thoughts kept coming back to the bandage on Cybelle's arm and filed it under the thousand and one questions buzzing in her brain

CHAPTER SIX

"WE THOUGHT YOU'D never get here."
Jocelyn glanced up from her froth-
covered beverage.

Goddess, but she loved her monthly
bitch sessions with the girls. Lucia had
taken the old Block and Tackle bar and
turned it into Lucia's Botanicals and
Brews, a place where they could all let

their hair down. It wasn't just beer, although she had some unique draughts on tap, it was the botanical potions and brews that drew people in.

In other words, it was a bar for witches.

And it was freaking fantastic.

Orlo was a kitchen witch and his food rivaled anything she could get anywhere else in town, no matter if it was a steak, a fig vinaigrette salad, or a basket of onion rings. The man had talent. If she actually leaned that way, she would be tempted to marry him just to have him cook for her the rest of her life.

But sadly, he and his husband were happily married and adopting a baby girl. A tiny little part of her was jealous, but they'd all made their choices. Even if hers left her a little lonely at the end of the day.

Love was for other people. Hers had left town with little explanation, but deep down she thought she knew. Being trapped into a relationship wasn't cool, and Kate had tried to do just that.

Warning her that it was close to a full moon, she'd seduced her right into bed, and when Devi accidentally marked her, it had been a bittersweet gift. It tied them together forever, but it also scared her off.

Goddess, she'd been an idiot.

Seven years later, she couldn't get the cat out of her mind and no other familiar would do.

Loneliness was a bitch. But she didn't blame Devi. All she'd ever wanted was to be a cop and to help people. Staying in Bixby and just being a familiar wasn't something in her blood. Especially with her family's bullshit kicking up dust. She had a lot to prove. Demon magic left a stain, even when she wasn't the one using it.

People had choices. And she wasn't going to stand in her way if leaving was what she wanted.

Her thoughts drifted back to the present as a steaming basket of onion rings drifted under her nose.

"Earth to Kate…"

The small table was laden with potato skins, cheese sticks, and now a heaping basket of onion rings with a vat of ranch that earned a happy grumble from her tummy and reminded her that she hadn't eaten much since breakfast.

But that was fine with her. All the better to enjoy the food, drinks, and atmosphere.

The lighting was dim, just like she liked it, but the plants Grace helped Lucia cultivate to share the space were especially suited to thrive and give the place an even more unique edge.

"I know. Sorry. It's been a hell of a day," Kate responded, taking her seat on the high bar stool.

"Tell me about it." Grace winced. "The garden shop was overrun with Karens and Chads and I ran out of succulent dirt."

"The world is indeed ending." Lucia made her way over, a large beer mug overflowing with goodness on her tray. "Here you go, Kate. You look like you could use this."

"Yes. Thank you." She grabbed at the mug with greedy fingers and sucked down a large gulp, the heady, malted brew like heaven on her tongue.

She loved the ladies at the store, but just soaking in the silence was a welcome change. If only her thoughts would follow. She was worried about Kendall and her visit with Cybelle had done nothing to assuage her fears. Frankly, they'd only added to them.

"I'm glad you could all make it. Especially tonight." Lucia set down the tray and climbed onto the last bar stool. Her dark eyes flashed with something like concern and Kate put her drink down with a *thunk*.

"What's happened?"

"That's what I wanted to talk to you about. The Council sent out a notice for all members to use caution in their travels."

"What does that mean?"

"There's been a rash of missing witches in town tonight and I wanted to see if you'd noticed anything odd."

Kate nibbled on her lip, unsure of how to respond. Eying the others, she took a deep breath and decided it was better to just get it over with.

"Well...Kendall didn't show up last night. Or today."

"Is she prone to that kind of behavior?"

"No." Kate shook her head. "She's been reliable, actually. Helpful to the max."

Lucia nodded, her gaze flickering to the other two.

"Anything strange going on with you?"

"Nope. Unless you count Melissa

Rodriguez not showing up to get her bakery order. The woman is like clockwork. But tonight, not a thing."

"Hmmm. Grace?"

"No. Just the usual, I'm afraid."

Lucia nodded. "Okay. Word from the other covens in town is something is going on. At least two of their younger members have gone missing in the last few hours. If Kendall is part of this, then we have at least three."

"I don't really know about Melissa. She's never mentioned a thing."

"Keep your ears open. If I were you, I would call it an early night."

"Well, that's kind of hard to do."

"I know. But listen...I overheard one of the patrons talking about a couple of dead teenagers behind the coffee place earlier tonight. They're still working the case, but they might be part of the witching community."

"Oh no." Grace pressed her lips together. "That's right down the road from the shop."

"No kidding." Jocelyn frowned. Her pottery studio was only a few blocks away as well.

"Just, everyone keep an ear to the ground, okay?" Lucia sighed and met Kate's eyes. "What?"

"So, Kendall went to the swamp to meet someone who wanted a spell."

"Oh, Goddess." Lucia closed her eyes. "That place is off limits for a reason. Has been for years."

Jocelyn snorted. "You all know the kids will always go hiding where they think we can't see. Hell, we did it."

"We did. But it wasn't teeming with

off energy back then, either."

"True."

"I sent a searcher spell but it hasn't come back yet," Kate said, pulling her hair behind her ear.

"Girl, be careful. I don't like the things I'm hearing." Grace's lips thinned into a line.

"I don't want any of you taking chances. At least not until we get more info from the powers that be."

Kate didn't either, but as they dissolved for the night, she knew exactly where she was headed, like it or not.

Her spelled blade burned a hole in her pocket, and she grit her teeth. Something wasn't right and she was going to find out what it was.

CHAPTER SEVEN

"ARE YOU GOING to change back, or am I going to have to live with the smell of wet cat in my car?"

Cappelli glared down at her, and Devi proceeded to rub her face in the towel Avery brought from the house. They were still by the water, and the scent of magic drifting through the air was really making her nuts. She really needed a shower, but that was going to have to wait.

"She hasn't shifted like this before," Avery commented. "Not at a crime scene."

Devi glared up at him, annoyed that whatever happened in the water had forced a change. In front of her old boss and temporary partner, no less.

"Well, she better get her butt back in human form because we still have another one to go and I don't intend to babysit an oversize housecat all night."

Hello... she wanted to say. But all she could do was hiss and pin back her ears. The thought of scratching her just to watch her bleed held some merit, but well... she didn't want to take the chance if the woman was actually human.

Infecting someone with shifter traits wasn't a good plan, even if she felt like dumping her ass head first into the swamp to see how she liked it.

"The swamp. You head out. I'll finish up here. Devi, let me know if you piece any of this together. The crew has already started working the scene, so you might want to get a move on." Avery was already moving toward a group of technicians.

Cappelli nodded. "Will do. From the preliminaries, it sounded like a rave gone wrong. But now, I'm not so sure."

"Keep me in the loop, will you?" He barely looked in her direction.

"No problem, sir."

A pair of eyes trained on Devi, and she fought the urge to squirm.

Her animal wanted to hunt, but she

forced herself to focus.

The shift was painful, her muscles already tired from her previous change. Her clothes lay in a sodden heap at the edge of the water, and all she had was the towel she was swathed in.

"Well, this is awkward."

"No kidding." Devi peeled a blob of wet, silvery white tresses off her face and wrapped the towel around her.

Nothing like being naked in front of your co-workers. It ranked high up on the fuck-this-shit list.

She had to move, but every part of her body protested.

Getting to her feet was a monumental task, but she did it. "I need you to take me to the nearest gas station. I need to change."

A half hour later, they were back on

the road, her damp mop of silver hair still smelling of swamp water and death.

Devi pressed her face against the passenger's door and sighed.

She didn't want to do this one. Something about it rang a little too close to home. And after the last stop in the suburbs, she was ready to hit the bar and down a few. Or curl up on her bed in the hotel room and shut out the world for a while.

Why had she scented Kate over the water? She hoped Gambian hadn't tracked her down already.

Kate had to be safe or she would lose her ever loving mind.

She picked up her phone, debating whether she should be the one to break the silence, and put it down again.

Damn it.

She snatched up the phone and before she could talk herself out of it, sent Kate a text.

Something's going down in the swamp. Felt your magic. Please be safe.

Goddess, her head was going to explode.

What the fuck had the woman been thinking?

Drowning herself in the swamp right in front of her?

The whole thing was fucked up and it was starting to mess with her head.

There was a reason she was good at this job, but damn, she had enough scars, damn it. She didn't need more.

Avery and Cappelli had caught up to her when she was hip deep in the water herself. The siren song of the deep had been calling and she didn't want to think about what might have happened if they hadn't gotten there when they did.

She'd grabbed her bag and changed while Cappelli filled up the car.

Cappelli opened the driver's side door and got behind the wheel without looking at her.

"What is wrong with you?"

"Excuse me?" Devi stuttered, blinking at the vehemence in her voice.

"You're my partner, for tonight at least. Like it or not, I need to know if you're going to get suicidal, or whatever the hell that was, with every tough case we work."

"No."

"Well, what was that?"

"I honestly don't know."

And she didn't. One minute she had been on the shore, and the next she was wading deep into the water.

"So, you always keep a change of clothes in your bag?"

"It's kind of the nature of the beast."

Cappelli winced.

"I know. Bad joke. But it kind of applies, don't you think?"

"I guess."

It was going to be a long night.

"Need some coffee?" Cappelli started the car, waiting for her answer.

"No. Let's just get this over with."

"Suit yourself."

Devi scooped her silvery white hair up into a messy up do and uncapped her rarely used lipstick. She stared at the crimson shade, her mind traveling back to when Kate first gave her the silver tube.

Kate.

Goddess she missed her.

It had been three years, but the sting of it still felt like yesterday.

Yeah. And whose fault was that?

Every time she picked the lipstick up, the zip of Kate's magic flowed over her like kisses on her skin and she was lost.

Bitterness twisted in her gut.

She had been damned if she did, and damned if she didn't.

Being a cop meant being her own person, not an extension of someone else. But no one understood and she had no choice but to walk. away.

So why did she still miss her so fucking much?

Her ocelot scowled at her from within. Of course, she knew.

The lipstick grew warm in her hand, and the memories of that last night played over in her mind as if it were yesterday.

"You look sexy in that shade of red." *Kate entered the room with a small object in her hand. The florescent glow of the bathroom lights brought out the silvery blue in her eyes and the chestnut waves of her hair.*

All ready for their night, Kate was a knockout in her blue slip of a dress.

"Thanks." Devi zipped up the side panel on the dress and adjusted her cleavage. Her breasts filled out the top portion of the crimson velvet bodice to a tee. Her long, silvery white hair was styled in old fashioned, large curls and parted down the middle, letting her shiny locks flow in waves down her back. One glance at her girl and her pulse pounded in her throat. "Are you sure we have to

go?"

Her animal agreed. She could still taste her, and the scent of her was everywhere.

They needed to talk about what happened earlier, but Devi was struggling to find the words.

Kate laughed, her lips curling up into a guarded smile. "You just want me all to yourself."

She wasn't wrong.

If they went out tonight, she would be sharing her and that was something she didn't want to do. Her body was still flush with heat from their earlier lovemaking and the unforgettable moment when she'd slid her teeth into Kate's neck, just under her hair.

The warm bloom of the mate bond had flooded through her, and when she'd pulled away, she found Kate's eyes closed.

A single tear slipped down her cheek.

"I won't hold you to it, you know," she whispered. "I know you don't want this."

The denial had been on Devi's lips, but she tasted the lie for what it was before it escaped.

Kate deserved more than that. She deserved someone who wasn't tied to demon magic, as much as she fought it.

Instead, she rose from the bed and shut herself in the bathroom and let the shower drown out her tears.

It wasn't fair.

Why did everything have to have rules and consequences?

Why couldn't she just love who she loved and have a life without all the bullshit?

If they came out publicly as a couple, she would be bound to Kate as a familiar and as much as signing her a death sentence if Gambian found a way to escape the box she'd sealed her in.

She had just started her job on the force and found her path to freedom.

Devi's eyes met Kate's in the mirror. She'd hit home and Kate immediately frowned.

Cops and witches didn't get along, let alone them knowing she was a familiar. It was well known Devi's family were hereditary familiars to some of the highest witching and demon families and it had taken her a long time to help them see her as a cop, not a supernatural freak they had to worry about.

What was she going to do?

Take her mate to every crime scene?

Call her when things got tough so she could funnel her power?

Keep her with her twenty-four hours a day to make sure some random demon didn't hand her over to Gambian just out of spite?

Fuck no.

She was no one's battery. And that was the argument that started and ended it all. And she couldn't stand by and watch while Kate's life was destroyed by something that wasn't in her control.

"I'm sorry Devi. I know your mom is still really pissed at you for quitting the coven. And I hardly ever see you anymore between you moving to the city and the yarn shop." Kate wrapped her arms around Devi and kissed her on the cheek. "I thought going tonight would be good for us. You used to love thumbing *your nose at what everyone else is expecting."*

They expected her to stay away.

They would be right.

"Sure. But tonight, I just wanted it to be us. Here. Together," Devi protested. If Kate wanted to go, then she would, but the last thing she wanted to do was be out in public and deal with other people's expectations, witch or otherwise.

"Just dinner with the coven, okay? Your mother is expecting us. Mine too. After that, we can go dancing." Kate's lips quirked into a flirty smile that faded when she took in Devi's expression. "We don't have to, I mean. If you really don't want to."

And she didn't.

Despite the risks they were taking just by being together, she didn't want to hurt her. Every time they touched, there was a very real possibility the goddess would bind them.

Witch and familiar.

Mates.

Which she had gone and done tonight.

Fuck.

Goddess, she was so stupid.

In her heart, she knew there would never be another for her. But in her head, she balked at the shackles they kept trying to put on her. Demon or otherwise.

Being a detective was a hard job and one that didn't follow a nine to five schedule.

How was she supposed to be a good mate in that reality?

"The coven knows full well why I left." *A slow burn of anger began to simmer in her gut. Her mother found ways to ruin*

everything even after she was dead. First her coven family, and now her time with her girlfriend. She jerked the back off the earring and fastened it, repeating the action with the other ear. Two diamonds sparkled back at her in the glass.

Her mother had never approved of her wanting to become a detective, or anything other than a bond between a witch and a familiar. She might as well have told to stay barefoot and pregnant. That was how she felt. Even if that person was Kate.

Why couldn't she just be left alone to live her life?

But the one thing Devi never wanted to do was hurt Kate, and if she was honest, and told her how she felt, that's exactly what would happen.

"Are we going to talk about it?" Kate

put her hand on her arm.

"No." Devi sighed. There were no words that wouldn't make things worse. "I want to enjoy the night."

"So, let's get out of here." Kate looped her arms around her and held out a small silver tube. "This is for you."

As her fingers reached around the lipstick, a zing of something she recognized as Kate's magic kissed her skin.

Too bad it was as bittersweet as the look she gave her as they walked out the door.

That was the last night they spent together.

She hadn't called. Neither had Devi.

It was just too fucking raw.

Seven years had gone by and she wasn't any closer to getting over it.

The car stopped and it jolted Devi out of her memories and back into reality.

"Jesus." The normal Texas landscape of pine trees and occasional oaks had shifted into shadowy swamplands. Her skin prickled with unease, her inner cat's ears turning down in disapproval.

The night seemed deeper here. But not like it used to.

It almost seemed...alive.

Devi didn't like it one bit.

"I know this place." It popped out of her lips before she could take it back and wanted to curse herself for it.

"Oh?"

"I used to live around here." That was all she was going to say. Cappelli kept to herself and she would take her cues and do the same.

All the witching families in Bixby had

forbidden anyone from going beyond the barrier of the swamps.

That didn't mean everyone listened. It was the top choice for teenagers longing to have a bit of freedom away from prying eyes. Pop up raves had been common. One site in particular snagged her memory.

A stolen kiss.

Bonfires snapping and crackling against the darkness.

A mutual discovery of bodies and groping hands.

It had been a time of awakening. But it was over now.

"What exactly was the complaint?"

"Neighbors at the edge of the swamp complained of a loud party. Then, they heard screams." Cappelli pulled the car over to the side of the road.

Bullshit.

"Nobody lives near enough to hear that."

Except maybe the recently dead Skyler Chambers. She'd have to check her phone records.

Cappelli shrugged. "What I don't understand is why they asked for us when we've already had three scenes tonight and the team is already on site."

"Did he say anything else?"

"No. Just that he needed a report asap."

"Shit. Where are Murray and Daniels?"

"They're working the homicide at the Pickled Bear."

It figured. People had damn near lost their minds being in lockdown for almost a year. It seemed like it was only getting worse.

Goddess, she was tired.

"Great."

Cappelli's lips curved into a smile. "Come on. Let's get this over with." Opening the driver's side door, she stepped out into the darkness.

Devi followed suit. She got out of the car and from the moment her feet touched the earth, she felt the vibration in her bones.

"Shit."

"What?"

"You don't feel that?"

For a moment, she wished Kate were here, then gave herself a mental slap. This was why she had to leave. The witch, familiar bond was too strong and they'd gotten too close to the fire.

Had she imagined her scent when she

was at the Chamber's house? It seemed like it was impossible, but she knew her magic anywhere. So where was it coming from and why would she be out here of all places?

"Feel what?"

Devi sighed. She really hated breaking in a new partner.

"How are you on a taskforce that deals with paranormal shit if you can't feel it?"

"At least I don't cut and run when things get tough."

"Go on." Devi crossed her arms, her lips twisted into a smirk. "Tell me how I have to *run* back here to help you do your job."

"You're a bitch."

"Right back atcha." Devi gave her a cold smile and turned her focus to the darkness beyond. Cappelli was noise. What was out there...it was a threat and she took it seriously.

"There's something here. And it feels...wrong." There wasn't any other way to say it.

Just then a ghost of music drifted toward them and she cocked her head.

"Before you ask, yes, I heard that."

Why hadn't the team turned off the music?

"Let's go."

"After you."

"Hang on." Devi went to the trunk of the car and dragged her duffle bag over. Yanking out a Taser, she tucked it into the waistband of her jeans. Her knife was heavy in her pocket, pulsing with each burst of energy.

There was no doubt about it. The very

land was alive.

She gave the tree line a visual sweep, the sense of not being alone washed over her.

"You want a flashlight?"

"No. I can see just fine, thanks."

Devi sighed. Let the games begin.

"Are you going to tell me what you are?"

A snort was her answer.

"You're a detective. Figure it out." With that, her mysterious new partner stalked off into the night and Devi was left to follow in her footsteps.

God.

The night couldn't be over fast enough.

CHAPTER EIGHT

KATE PULLED UP to the old rave site
and sure enough, Kendall's car was
there. But so were at least a dozen
others and what appeared to be a
sheriff's car and a crime scene tech van.
Rolling the window down, she was hit
with the fetid slap of cool, moisture-
laden air, the spell she sent out still

mysteriously silent.

Something was way wrong.

The flesh on her arms tightened, and gooseflesh settled in.

If there were police here, why couldn't she hear sirens and all the crap that comes with a crime scene?

She watched TV.

No... this was... off.

Where were the cops?

What had they come here to find?

Her phone buzzed and she gave it a cursory glance. Then, she looked at it again.

Devi?

Something's going down in the swamp. Felt your magic. Please be safe.

What the hell?

She sat back in her seat, irritation warring with worry. This...this was what she said after seven fucking years?

Then her stomach dropped.

Was she in trouble?

Her heart raced and she struggled to get her emotions under control.

Devi was back?

And at the swamp, no less?

She hadn't sensed her yet, but she hadn't been trying either.

Parking the car, she got out, her feet loud on the pebbled ground. She remembered when they'd snuck out here as teenagers to put the rocks down so their cars didn't keep getting stuck in the mud. She and Devi had laughed and gotten tangled up in each other more than once that night.

Just the thought of her made her pulse quicken, but then she forced herself to shake it off. They'd each made their choice and they were going to have to live with it. If she was here, it had to do with work and that made her nervous.

The tree line was dark with unknown menace and it made her skin crawl. Dark magic fairly drenched the place and it made her want to take a shower. What the hell was going on around here?

"Kendall? Devi?" Kate called out, her voice jarring her amid the silence.

The only sounds were the chirping cicada's and the wind whispering through the trees.

Her fingertips tingled as she made her way toward the rave site just a little way beyond the parking area. They'd cleared the land just enough to have bonfires and have some fun, but not enough to take away from the nature beauty of the swamp.

Eyes adjusting to the dark, she carefully made her way between the brush, taking care not to make any noise.

What she saw made her freeze in her tracks.

CHAPTER NINE

WHAT MUST HAVE been minutes felt like hours as Devi stumbled around in the brush. They still hadn't apprehended anything but a shrub and a moss-covered log that Devi could have sworn was staring at her. Vines slid across the ground, and plants brushed against her, like they were taking a taste.

Goddess, but she hated this part of the swamp.

She came here as a teen, just to prove she could. But damn, she never remembered it being this creepy before. And why hadn't they driven around to find the parking area they'd built as kids for the raves?

"Better to go in the back way," was all Cappelli had said. "The team will probably do the same."

Except she hadn't seen a sign of them.

Not one.

Well, shit.

Let's fucking do things the hard way.

Moving plants and trees with eyes?

No.

Even with all the booze she'd downed, she'd have remembered that shit.

She was jumpy, and the worst part was Cappelli knew it.

"You okay back there?"

"Fine," she bit out as another branch tickled her face.

She would be better off if she could just shift and let her ocelot take the reins. Her animal would have found whatever was messed up and they'd be out of here eating breakfast in an hour.

Her cat stretched beneath her skin, eager to do just that. But this was a situation that called for her to stay in human form. Besides, she didn't know her new partner well enough to trust her. She knew she was a shifter. Let her wonder about the rest.

If she wanted to be cagey, Devi could play along.

The sound of a twig breaking nearby

made her freeze. A low growl bubbled up her throat and she scanned the shadows.

Her partner was nowhere in sight.

Fuck.

"Cappelli," she hissed.

But the night had taken her as if she had never been there.

Double fuck.

She eyed the trees and put her hands on her hips.

"Really?"

She half expected the old cypress to shoot her the bird. Huffing, she rolled her eyes and peered once again into the shadows.

She grit her teeth and moved forward. Her partner hadn't vanished; she had probably just gone ahead to scope things out.

It was the music that lured her deeper into the congested mire of moss-covered cypress trees. The heart of the swamp loomed dark, the cicadas chirping blending with the strange echo of something melodic and infectious. Dank wet air pawed against her face and she swiped at the perspiration trickling down her forehead.

A shadow moved into her line of sight and she couldn't help but breathe an irritated sigh of relief.

Her temporary partner traipsed through the brush ahead her in the inky black. The pale light of the moon was the only light saving her from stepping into a bog or worse, a gator trap. Cappelli had taken a chance leading the way, but if she wanted to stumble around in unfamiliar territory, it wasn't up to Devi to tell her what to do.

The blade she carried whispered to her beneath the confines of her jeans pocket. It had awakened the moment they'd stepped foot on this cursed earth and she knew better than to take anything around her for granted.

The decorative knife was similar to ones you'd find at expensive jewelry shops in the hoity-toity shopping districts of town, except for the strange green fire twisted through the metal of the blade. Sometimes, when she looked at it, she could swear there were faces there.

Usually after a couple of beers.

Her position within the department was a tenuous one. People distrusted things they didn't understand and she was exactly that. It wouldn't help that she'd been dragged back to her hometown to solve whatever it was that was happening here.

She would do her job and go home to her empty apartment just like she always did. And she didn't have a death wish. Playing with fire was fun but when you landed in the flames, too...well now. That left singe marks. She had a job to do. Weird shit was happening and they paid her to figure it out with as little body count as possible.

She thought about the 911 call that Cappelli played on the way to the scene.

"Oh my God. Come now! They're killing her!" The caller dropped the phone with a clatter. After a moment and the sounds of labored breathing the voice resumed. "It came out of the swamp Holy crap! Kill it. You have to..."

RED MOON RISING

A terrible scream almost made Devi jump and the line went dead.

Cappelli had met her eyes, steering the car toward the reported area of the incident. She'd responded to the homicide team there would be a slight delay in their arrival. If it was anything like she thought, it was a party gone bad and someone was playing a prank on a snitch once they found her on the phone. Now here they were in the middle of the swamp hunting down clues like some kind of episode of True Detective.

Where was the rest of the team?

She didn't like this.

Not one bit.

"You see anything?" She whispered.

"Not yet."

Something glimmered in the shadows ahead. She knew better than to trust anything out here. Swamp gas did funny things. The music grew louder. Instead of an electronica beat, this music brimmed with percussion and the blood rush of orchestrated screams. The sound sent shivers down Devi's spine.

"Do you see the lights?"

Cappelli moved next to Devi, her narrow face white in the faint glow of the moon. Her lips pressed together and she nodded. "This reminds me of a bust I did a few years back. Looked like an episode of that swamp justice show. There was some pretty nasty voodoo activity on site."

"Voodoo? Like what?" Devi sucked in a deep breath. She'd seen a few things at the local tourist traps since she took the job at the department, but nothing that rivaled what life would have been like if she'd stayed. There was a reason she left home. Other people's darkness was always preferable to one's own.

Cappelli urged her forward, a faraway look on her expressive face. "Yeah. Dead chickens scattered everywhere. An eviscerated goat...and the snakes. God, I hate those damned snakes."

Devi nodded. It sounded familiar to the occult scenes she'd worked in the city. As much as it turned the stomach of the cop she'd been before, it electrified her animal.

"We have to finish this or Avery will have our asses. I don't know why he insisted you consult, but whatever."

Devi didn't say a thing. All they had to do was get through this shift and she could go home. That was the deal and she was sticking with it.

"Capote and Ford are in Slidell checking out info on that stranded camper they found last week." Cappelli peered into the shadowy forest of hanging moss and cypress trees.

"Right." Her foot slipped in a pile of slimy putrescence and she shuddered. One time in the swamp was all it took to learn to wear boots.

"Where'd they find the camper?" She shook her foot and didn't bother looking down. The jeans more than likely ruined, too.

"A mile or so away."

The music stopped and their steps sounded loud in the sudden silence.

"Come on." Cappelli picked up the pace, tugging on the sleeve of her suit jacket.

Devi jerked back without even

thinking.

"Sorry." She slid her gaze away, bolting ahead of Devi into the murky night.

Her breath came in soft pants, she hurried after Cappelli, brush and scrub pawing at her clothes and face. The light grew brighter but it barely registered as she struggled to keep up, slamming into Cappelli's back when she froze.

Images from Cappelli's past assailed her. A crime scene hovered and centered in her vision and she cursed herself for not paying closer attention.

A dead girl in a white dress laid out on the ground, her eyes open and glassy. The altar flickered with candlelight, the pavement surrounding it covered with colorful chalk marks and symbols. Entrails in wooden bowls covered in flies buzzed and the warehouse smelling of blood and feces.

She also felt the other woman's pain.

But the memories weren't over.

Her partner darted out in front of her trying to deflect the bokur coming at her from the far reaches of the shadowy room with a machete. Ridgeway, all too human and still recovering from medical leave, wasn't fast enough. The sickening sound of the blade imbedding in his flesh caused her fragile stomach to heave once more.

"Ridgeway!" She croaked out, staggering forward. She drew for her gun in time to aim and fire, hoping to God she connected with something that counted. That something was the bokur's head. It exploded, the sound echoing through the cavernous structure.

Shit.

A hiss greeted her and red eyes flashed in the darkness.

"Get out of my head," Cappelli bit out, stepping away.

Devi dug her nails into her palms to bring her focus back into the physical world.

A flash of fang revealed, and she understood. Her new partner was a vampire, and she'd been through the shit. Part of her wondered where Ridgeway was now, but hell if she was going to ask.

Devi swallowed, nervous perspiration erupting all over her body. She had gotten used to thinking of her as human. Having a reaction to her wasn't planned and she had to shake herself.

"Shit. I'm sorry."

Devi was drawn back into Cappelli's consciousness and memories as her own nausea took over and Cappelli's attempt to keep the contents of her stomach from defiling the crime scene was lost. The sour tang of bile overwhelmed her as she stumbled away and retched into the dirt.

"Ugh." Her face was hot and she wiped at her mouth with the back of her hand. "Nasty."

Devi let out a strangled breath and blinked to clear the visual from her mind.

"Hey," Cappelli grunted, turning her body to help steady her.

Oh God.

Devi held up her hand.

"Please don't touch me again. I don't want to see anything else. I'm okay."

"So that's why he wanted you."

"Among other things," Devi grunted and tried to right herself, but instead got an eyeful of the rave site.

She tried to keep the tremor out of her voice as her eyes adjusted to the light. The scene in front of them was carnage. A campfire burned and within it she could see the charred remains of something that appeared more or less human.

More images of her past experience with the occult came unbidden and she had to blink them away. There were reasons she'd been asked to come here. She may hate it, but she was good at her job.

"It's a body."

"And not just one."

Bodies of bound teenagers lay around

the fire, their throats slit. The pooling blood appeared black in the dim light. One kid, a boy, was sporting a hat that looked like a house from Hogwarts. Her fingers itched to touch him, but she feared the visions it would bring. Perhaps she wouldn't need to.

This was familiar. Like a scene from one of her case studies. A few more seconds of observation and the facts fell into play.

Isolation.

Swamp.

Elements of magic.

It was all there. Hell, she could even read the plot right now, it was so textbook.

Corpses of slain uniformed officers, what appeared to be a detective and a couple of crime scene techs, lay among the witches.

Some were mauled, but others had their throats slit.

She said the word before the thought even processed. "Power."

"What?"

"The hat the kid is wearing. It's a magical wanna be." Devi took in the rest of the scene, nausea pooling in her gut. "You know? Like charging a battery?"

"Not something we've seen much of around here, detective."

"But I bet you have in your own circles." She let her gaze linger over Cappelli's and the woman's icy façade melted just a little.

"It's happened before. Vampires drinking those with power to take their essence."

"Witches do it, too."

But among the ravers lay the missing members of the homicide team, their throats torn open, eyes staring blankly into the night.

"Cappelli. Oh, no."

"I see them."

"This is seriously fucked."

A shadowy figure burst out of the woods, darting toward them at breakneck speed. He was covered in gore, his eyes wide with terror.

"Get out of here! It's coming."

"Andrews?" Cappelli backed up a step, her mouth open in shock. "What happened to the team?"

"Go!" Andrews roared. His right arm was drenched in blood, a bite wound laying open his flesh.

Devi moved on impulse, the blade she carried under the suit jacket freed by virtue of muscle memory and a will to survive. Something was chasing him and she didn't want that something to clamp down on her.

Cappelli stepped into the panicked officer's path. "Jesus, Andrews. Stop." She reached out to detain him but he maneuvered out of her grip.

"No," he moaned. "Not going to become that."

He gave Cappelli a mournful look.

"Leave this place before you die." Then he dove head first into the bonfire.

"Stop! What the fuck are you doing, man?" Cappelli tried to pull him from the fire, but it was more than a little too late. The inferno grew, engulfing him in flames.

"Leave him." Devi broke her own rule and touched the vampire, this time putting up her shields.

"He was one of the best in the department. None of this shit makes any sense." She thrust her fingers through her hair in frustration.

"We have to know what to look for. And if whatever was chasing him is still out there, we better be ready."

Without a word, Devi sheathed her weapon and pressed down the radio call button. "This is Graves and Benoit requesting a bus and backup. Multiple victims on site. Officers down. I repeat, officers down."

Nothing else in the macabre scene moved. Whoever else performed the rite was long gone. It was a wasteland of death and destruction. She walked along the edge of the campfire and noted the strange markings on the stones.

RED MOON RISING

Runes.

Sigils.

All meant for drawing power.

A bloody pentagram drawn in the dirt enclosed the space, and the fire burned in the middle like a beacon in the night. The smell of sulfur was unmistakable, but faded.

On the ground lay a discarded copy of the Necronomicon. It was the kind of cheap paperback you'd find at any chain bookstore. Well-thumbed and covered in bloody fingerprints, it was a spell of intent. There, hidden in the sand, were the complex drawings she was looking for. In the shadows of the trees, she found the twin scythe moons and a throne-like chair between them.

She thought back to the 911 call and shuddered.

Movement caught her eye and she gripped her blade and almost dropped it.

Kate appeared out of the darkness, her scent wrapping around her like smoke.

CHAPTER TEN

KATE BLINKED IN the darkness, almost unable to believe what she was seeing.

Devi.

She was here.

She'd felt her essence, but wasn't sure if it was real, or just a ruse.

Without even thinking, she stepped from the shadows.

"Hello?"

"Witch." A vampire approached, not even bothering to hide her fangs.

"Devi?" Kate licked her lips, then stifled a gasp as her gaze slid past her mate to the scene beyond.

"Kate. What are you doing here?" Devi stared at her; eyes wide. Her animal was close to the surface and Kate could sense her fear. She could also feel the link between their matching daggers.

"Kendall, a girl from the shop, went missing. I traced my spell here but…"

"You need to leave. Now," the vampire hissed. "This is an active crime scene."

"What?"

"Jesus, Cappelli." Devi shot the other woman a vicious glare.

"She's a witch." Cappelli growled, taking a threatening step forward.

"Maybe she's controlling whatever attacked Andrews."

Devi rounded on the vampire; her fangs elongated.

"*She's* my mate."

Kate swallowed, her knees growing weak. Were her ears playing tricks on her? Had the words she'd been waiting to hear for seven years just erupted out of Devi's mouth or had she just lost her mind?

"Prove it."

"Excuse me. I'm still here."

"I don't have to prove anything to you, vamp girl. She's not the threat here."

"Like I said. Prove it. For all I know, she's that fucking demon that killed James all tucked up in a pretty package just to lure you in."

Devi stared at the vampire as if she'd been slapped.

"Demon? What is she talking about?"

"Nothing. Look. It's about my old partner."

"What?" Kate blinked, not entirely sure what was going on.

"I'm waiting." The vampire edged her suit jacket back to reveal a gun at her hip. She fingered the safety and looked pointedly at Kate.

"Fine." Devi spun back around and before she realized what was happening, captured Kate's lips in a kiss.

Kate meant to shove her away. This wasn't something she wanted to share in front of anyone, especially, after seven years of silence and guilt, worrying that she tried to trap the one thing that was good in her life.

But the warm and spicy scent of her lover filled her with happiness and a groan slipped from her lips, despite trying not to react.

Devi was the first to draw back.

"Hi."

"Hi, yourself." Even to her own ears, her voice sounded breathless. But then she let herself see. "The ground is..." she couldn't even form the words.

Nodding, Devi sighed. "It looks like someone lured them here and took their power."

"Not to mention murdered them all," the vampire interjected, her gaze still radiating hostility.

"I should go look for Kendall."

"No." Devi swallowed and blocked her way. "If she's there, she's gone."

Tears prickled the corners of her eyes

and she angrily brushed them away. "Who would do this?"

"You're the witch. You tell us."

"I don't know. But I'm going to find out."

CHAPTER ELEVEN

DEVI SWALLOWED, STILL staring at Kate.

She was here.

The blade in her pocket pulsed, recognizing its twin close by.

"There are police already here. And dead. What happened?" Kate peered at the bonfire, wrinkling her nose in distaste as the wind shifted direction and she caught the smell of burning flesh.

"Have you heard anything from the witches?" Devi asked. Goddess, but she had to try and focus on the case.

Nodding, Kate rubbed her hands on her jeans. Her eyes looked tired, Devi realized.

"I just left the store. You know, the one we talked about opening? Well, I met with some of the girls at Lucia's and there was talk about something going down."

"Lucia's?"

"Used to be the old bar on Main. I'll have to show you. If you're in town long enough..." her voice trailed off.

"So, even though they told you something was going down, you decided to come and check things out on your own?" Cappelli's eyebrows lifted.

"Kendall, one of my employees, didn't show for work. I sent out a finder spell, and it led me here."

"I felt you. At the last crime scene. The scent carried over the water." Devi was almost embarrassed to admit it.

"I got your text."

"You texted her? Are you nuts?" Cappelli growled. "What if she was a part of it?"

"Ladies. We have company."

A swirl of wind skittered around Kate, her chestnut hair swirling around her face as her element gathered strength. Her gaze shot to the darkness of the woods and Devi heard the crashing of brush and branches as a wolfen beast crashed into the open, heading straight for them.

"Kate!"

But her girl was already in action. Arms thrown wide, she whipped the tempests from teacups to tornados, hurling them at the creature.

Cappelli dove at it, struggling to subdue it, even with her superhuman strength. The creature shook her off, and Devi heard the unmistakable crack of her head hitting one of the large rocks near the fire pit.

Fuck.

"Why don't you tangle with someone your own size, asshole?" Her blade was in her hand before she even realized it and she took her place at Kate's side. Her gusts were getting fewer, and the creature was getting too close for comfort.

"Take what you need."

Kate's eyes met hers and she thought she saw a shimmer of something that looked like tears.

"I'm not going to use you. You have to do this because you want to."

It wasn't even a question.

But Devi didn't have time to answer. The beast was on her, grabbing her by the hair and throwing her toward the nearest tree.

Fuck.

She slammed into the bark and blinked, her face numb from pain, and her arm twisted at an off angle.

Double fuck.

Moving it gingerly, she scraped her body off the ground and stalked back toward the fray. Cappelli had risen and was holding the creature back, but one good jab and she lost her footing, and the beast lunged for Kate.

Devi lost her mind.

Nothing else mattered.

Not her job.

Not the demon.

It was only ever about Kate.

The shift happened without her thinking about it. Muscles reformed and bones crunched, but this time, she allowed Kate's power inside of her. They were one, and as one they were stronger.

And a fuck ton larger.

The snarl ripped from her chest, and she charged the beast. Claws out, she swiped at it, sending it sailing. Kate lay too still, her perfect skin marred by bloody furrows from the creature's claws.

Enraged, Devi stalked forward and

they met, claw for claw, fang for fang.

Pain didn't exist.

She was fighting for Kate's life. There was a connection, but it was growing fainter.

She had to end this.

Now.

"Get it to come to you," Cappelli snarled, heaving herself out of the dirt. Her suit hung in tatters, and she shrugged off the jacket in disgust.

Devi yowled as the beast crashed into her, but she held on, twisting her legs up around its neck. It struggled, but she dug deep.

"Hold it!" Cappelli stalked forward, her perfect blonde hair askew, eyes black with fury.

Jaws snapping, it tried to latch on, but Cappelli was faster, snapping its neck with a swift twist of her hands.

Releasing the creature, Devi couldn't tell whose blood she was covered in. But they'd won.

The beast was dead.

"Devi." She heard Kate whisper her name, but it sounded far away.

"She's lost a lot of blood."

Cappelli.

God.

She was such a b…

CHAPTER TWELVE

KATE SAT IN the ungodly hospital chair and watched the machines dance to Devi's heartbeat. She was bandaged and casted to the nth degree and Kate didn't know whether to scream or just crawl in bed beside her.

It wasn't fair.

She'd gotten the chance to see her,

only to almost lose her again.

Who was she kidding? The second she woke up, she'd be gone now that the beast was dead.

But it hadn't just been a beast.

She'd crawled over to cradle Devi's head in her lap as the vampire called in for medical support and watched as the grotesque animal shifted form.

Her gasp brought the vampire's attention back in her direction and her lips formed a grim line.

It had been Cybelle.

But that hadn't answered every question in her mind. The girl wasn't the type to think of all of this on her own.

And why would she kill her girlfriend?

Just because she sold some spells?

No.

It didn't make sense.

She tried to tell the vampire, but she was on the phone again talking with her supervisor. Not long after, the ambulance came and with it, a flurry of activity.

They tried to pry Devi from her arms but she wouldn't let them. And now here she was, waiting for her to wake up so she would at least know she was safe.

A blip from one of the machines brought her out of her head and she found herself looking into Devi's eyes.

"Hey."

"Hey yourself."

Devi gave her a half-hearted smile, then winced. "Where's Cappelli?"

"With the crime scene techs. They have a lot of work to do out there. That girl who killed those people, I knew her."

"I'm sorry."

"It doesn't make sense."

"I need to talk to Avery and Cappelli."

"They said to tell you they'd be in touch. And not to go anywhere."

"No doubt." She tried to sit up, but made another face. "Are you okay?"

"I've been better."

Her face still stung from the beast's claws, and she was sore from where she'd hit the ground, but otherwise fine.

The wind whispered inside of her and she reached for Devi, the need to touch her nearly overwhelming.

"I couldn't stand by and let it hurt you." Devi closed her eyes. "It didn't matter what happened to me."

Anger, sharp and hot, sizzled through her and with it, a tiny tempest of air swirled through the room, ruffling the clipboard on the end of the bed.

"Don't you dare say that." Tears prickled in Kate's eyes. "It does matter." She moved from the chair and perched on the edge of the bed.

"I left you."

There it was.

"And I tricked you into marking me, so we're even."

Devi's eyes snapped open. "What are you talking about?"

Shame crept hot up the back of her neck. "That night, I knew you were close to the moon, but I just wanted to be with you. It didn't matter about anything else. But when you marked me, I knew you didn't really mean it. That you wanted to leave. And I wasn't going to stop you."

"Kate."

"I'm sorry. I know we're technically mates, but I'm not going to hold you back. I never wanted that."

"I left to protect you."

"What?"

Devi fidgeted, tearing at one of the bandages on her face. "There. God. I couldn't see a damned thing."

"You're terrible."

"I know."

"So...elaborate, please?"

"You know my family history."

"Okay. Sure. Your mom was into demons."

"And she was killed by one. But not before she apparently bargained with one to save my life in exchange for a blood bond."

Ice shivered beneath Kate's skin.

"A blood bond?"

"It's a long story. James and I buried that damned box. I left to protect you, but now she's back and I'm going to lose you anyway."

"Wait. James? Who says I'm going anywhere?" Kate demanded. She took Devi's hand in hers.

"I can't lose you."

"Then don't, you idiot."

"We have a lot to figure out. And I'm not going to let her win."

"One step at a time. Okay? Besides, you still have to meet the others."

"Others?"

"The Circle. But we'll talk about that later."

She leaned over the bed and placed a tender kiss on Devi's lips. Energy crackled around them and a moan slid from between Kate's lips.

"I'm a mess," Devi protested.

"So am I."

She placed a kiss on her collarbone and slid the hospital gown out of the way. Kate gazed at her lover's voluptuous body and felt a warmth trickle in her secret places. Leaning forward, she placed a kiss on the raised scar that ran along her lover's abdomen.

"See. We're magic together."

"You're killing me."

"Am I?" Wisps of magic trailed along Devi's skin as Kate explored her beautiful imperfections.

"You are as lovely now as you were then."

Kate stood up and padded over to the door, locking it against wandering nurses. Visiting hours were almost over, so they didn't have long before someone would come along and try to kick her out.

Making short work of her clothes, she gently climbed onto the bed, mindful of Devi's injuries.

"Now." Kate pressed her lips to Devi's. Kissing her softly, she edged her thighs apart and sank between them.

Their nipples touched and sparks flew as hunger grew between them.

"I need you," Devi rasped.

Kate found her lips and traced the lines of her body, stroking and healing with each caress.

Breath coming heavier, Devi sighed against her and Kate delved lower.

Lips tingling, she explored her lover's flesh. Hungry for her touch, she let her fingers wander the soft, fleshy plane of her stomach and the fine line of the scar that still remained. It was part of her. That was all. She stroked it, another branch of the road map of her life.

"I love your breasts." Kate nipped the taut pink peaks and the sensation reverberated through her body.

Devi moaned and she moved between her thighs. Thrusting her fingers into the scalding heat of her molten core, Kate stroked the spark and coaxed her into an inferno.

"Oh God. Fuck me," Devi begged, her legs splayed wide. She thrust against Kate's hand, finally surrendering to her need.

Kate slid three fingers inside of Devi's channel, stretching her wide. Juices flowing, her lover arched her back as Kate began to pummel her, tweaking her erect clit as she moved. Pinching and fondling her breasts, Kate worked down Devi's body, finally spreading her wide open. Withdrawing her hand, she blew on her moist folds causing Devi to thrash and moan.

"Goddess, bless. Don't you dare stop now." She panted.

"Do you think I would dare?" Kate whispered into the flesh of her stomach. Licking and nibbling her way past the scar, she worked her way back to Devi's mound. Placing a kiss upon the neatly trimmed triangle, she gently parted Devi's folds and began to explore her with her tongue. Licking and sucking, she pulled Devi to the edge of the bed. Sinking her tongue deep inside of her, she fucked her. Swirling wide, Kate edged her clit further toward orgasm by bumping it with her nose.

"Oh God!" Devi shrieked. Her fingers pulled at Kate's dark curls, pushing her face against her throbbing clit.

Smiling, Kate pulled back and thrust three fingers deep inside of her. Her core spasmed around her fingers, and Devi shrieked, a keening cry echoing through the hospital room.

A knocking sound at the door brought Kate out of her happy delirium.

"Hello! This door isn't supposed to be locked."

Three more bangs and Kate started to giggle, staggering off the bed. Between them, Devi's wounds had almost healed and so had Kate's.

Magic.

Goddess, she loved it. Even if it did make her want to eat an entire blackberry pie.

She would look into that. After she got them home.

"You're awful. Gonna get me kicked out of the hospital."

"I don't think you need it now." Kate reached for her clothes, but wasn't fast enough.

The doorknob rattled and an angry nurse burst inside.

"What the..."

Kate couldn't hold it inside anymore. She snort laughed and let the sheet fall as the nurse shrieked and called for backup.

"Well, I guess you're staying at my place."

"Do I get the spare room?"

"Not on your life." Kate leaned in and kissed her. "But I think we're going to have to find you some pants."

Thank you for reading!

For more from The Silver Circle Witches, watch for Blue Moon Rising, Book Two to come in the spring 2023!

Turn the page for a preview from Blue Moon Rising now...

PREVIEW

LUCIA BELLFLOWER LET the door to the kitchen swing shut behind her, the noise of the bar fading into the chirping of crickets and other denizens of the night. Rain had started misting down, bringing her customers inside from the lakeside deck, and she figured she might as well get some of the trash out while there was a lull and it wasn't raining too hard.

She rolled the garbage can toward the dumpster, neatly hidden behind a wooden fence well covered with morning glory.

Her boots crunched along the walkway, the thump and bump of the trash bin wheels along the uneven path echoing in the near silence. It was a nice breather from the din inside, and she let the damp night sink into her soul.

Water was her element, and she didn't mind the rain. If anything, being out in it was refreshing, especially since she'd gotten off the call with the local coven.

"Idiots." She shook her head, using her irritation to fuel her movements. The scent of greasy, congealed food and heavy odor of trash hung in the air as she tossed the bags into the dumpster and slammed the lid shut.

Something was wrong in Bixby, but not one of the elders seemed to be lifting a fingernail to find out what it was and that just pissed her the hell off.

Witches had gone missing and there had been no explanation. It had been embarrassing to say the least when the Silver Circle girls had come in for their monthly bitch session and she couldn't tell them more than that.

Be careful.

Stay away from the swamp.

Watch your back.

She snorted, jerking the can back toward the path. Every witch in town knew the drill. The swamp was off limits. Hell, she could see it across the lake every day of her life.

Against her better judgment, she turned to look at the sinister form of trees. The last time she'd gone there, she'd been a teenager looking for a good time at one of the bonfires the local human kids liked to indulge in. Booze, drugs, magical shenanigans, and a whole lot of groping ran rampant.

It was also the night her mother vanished amid another cluster of disappearances. The coven hadn't had any answers for her then, either.

She shook her head, shame heating her cheeks.

Her mother would have never gone into the swamp if she hadn't been there. If she hadn't been so stubborn, thinking she knew better.

Rolling the wheely can as it wobbled

into an uneven spot on the path hidden by a puddle, she cursed, righting it.

Thinking about her mother wasn't a productive way to spend the few quiet moments she would have but she couldn't help the creeping sense of déjà vu when she clicked off the news.

Murders.

Disappearances.

That damned swamp.

Fifteen years and still not one clue as to where she'd gone.

But when she turned her gaze back toward the dark, she could swear she could hear something calling to her from beneath the waves.

A gurgle.

A plea.

Her task abandoned, she took a step toward the water and cocked her head, listening.

The energy was off. It had been for days, now. Last night had been the worst of it so far, but she refused to believe that was the start and end of it. Dark magic roamed the streets and witches were dying.

The questions was, what could she do about it?

Nothing seemed off in her clientele. Not even the shifters and their usual boisterous nature. Even Nina, one of the nurses in the neighboring town had popped in for a pint of O Negative with one of her fangy buddies and all seemed right with the world.

So, what the fuck was going on?

One thing she did know... someone knew something and she was damned well going to find out what it was.

A loud slam of a door snapped her out of her reverie. It didn't serve her well to stay out here alone. Tossing the garbage into the dumpster, she headed back into the noisy din of the bar, the long shadows of the trees looking on.

Watch for Blue Moon Rising at your favorite online retailer.

Don't forget to keep turning the pages to follow Erzabet and Gina as they team up to bring you many more delicious paranormal romance books in 2023 and check out their incredible back list!

ALSO BY GINA KINCADE

Speed Dating with the Denizens of the Underworld

Lucifer

Demi

Hera

Shadow Legacies

Hunter Moon

Ghost Moon

Blood Moon

Coming Soon!

RED MOON RISING

Born of Hellfire

Hellbound Heart

Demon's Playground

Devil's Mate

Shifting Hearts Dating App

Mistle Tie Me

Bear It All

Chocolate Moon Cafe

Your Wolfish Heart

Outfoxing Her Mate

Shifting Hearts Dating App: Books 1-3

Green Rock Falls

Accidentally Forever

CONNECT WITH GINA

Facebook

https://www.facebook.com/authorginakin
cade/

Newsletter Mailing List

https://landing.mailerlite.com/webforms/l
anding/r1r5n4

Twitter

https://twitter.com/ginakincade

RED MOON RISING

BookBub

https://www.bookbub.com/authors/gina-kincade

Blog/Webpage:

https://www.ginakincade.com/

Instagram

https://www.instagram.com/ginakincade/

Goodreads

https://www.goodreads.com/ginakincade

ABOUT GINA KINCADE

USA Today Bestselling Author Gina Kincade spends her days tapping away at a keyboard, through blood, sweat, and often many tears, crafting steamy paranormal romances filled with shifters and vampires, along with witchy urban fantasy tales in magical worlds she hopes her readers yearn to crawl into.

A busy mom of three, she loves healthy home cooking, gardening, warm beaches, fast cars, and horseback riding.

Ms. Kincade's life is full, time is never on her side, and she wouldn't change a moment of it!

Find more from Gina at: https://www.ginakincade.com/

CONNECT WITH ERZABET

Twitter

@erzabetbishop

Instagram

https://www.instagram.com/erzabetbishop/

Bookbub

https://www.bookbub.com/authors/erzabet-bishop

RED MOON RISING

Website and Newsletter

http://erzabetwrites.wix.com/erzabetbis
hop

Facebook Author Page

https://www.facebook.com/erzabetbish
opauthor

Goodreads

http://www.goodreads.com/author/sho
w/6590718.Erzabet_Bishop

Street team

https://www.facebook.com/groups/101
8269998190112/

ALSO BY ERZABET BISHOP

Speed Dating with the Denizens of the Underworld

Lucifer

Demi

Hera

Shadow Legacies

Hunter Moon

Ghost Moon

Blood Moon

Coming Soon!

RED MOON RISING

Born of Hellfire

Hellbound Heart

Demon's Playground

Devil's Mate

Shifting Hearts Dating Agency Series

Hedging Her Bets

Waking Up Wolf

Kitten Around

Shifting Hearts Dating Agency Collection

Books 1-3

Shifting Hearts Dating App Series

Mistle Tie Me

Your Wolfish Heart

Chocolate Moon Cafe

ERZABET BISHOP & GINA KINCADE

Bear It All

Outfoxing Her Mate

Shifting Hearts Dating App: Books 1-3

My Wicked Mates Series

Craving Her Mates

Surrendering to Her Mate

Tormenting Her Mate

My Wicked Mates Series Collection:
Books 1-3

Westmore Wolves Series

Wicked for You

Heart's Protector

Burning for You

Taming the Beast

Mistletoe Kisses

RED MOON RISING

Westmore Wolves Collection, Books 1-5

Curse Workers Series

Sanguine Shadows

Map of Bones

Malediction

Arcane

Curse Workers Collection: Books 1-3

Sigil Fire Series

Sigil Fire

Written on Skin

Glitter Lust

First Christmas: A Sigil Fire Holiday Romance

Sigil Fire Books 1-3: An Urban Fantasy Boxed Set

Collections and Anthologies

Holidays and More:

A Lesfic Short Story Collection

Lesfic Tales:

A Lesfic Short Story Collection

Sapphic Holiday Cruise:

A Lesbian Holiday Collection

Sweet Sensations:

A Short Story Anthology

Standalone Novels

Snow

ABOUT ERZABET BISHOP

ERZABET BISHOP IS A USA TODAY BESTSELLING and award-winning author of over forty paranormal and contemporary romance books. She lives in Houston, Texas, and when she isn't writing about sexy shifters or voluptuous heroines, she enjoys playing in local bookstores and watching movies with her husband and furry kids.

CPSIA information can be obtained
at www.ICGtesting.com
Printed in the USA
BVHW060021301222
655301BV00009B/210

9 781773 574486